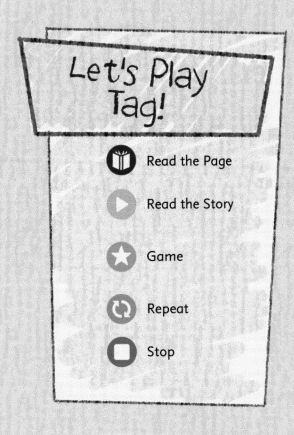

Let's Play Tag!

- 📖 Read the Page
- ▶ Read the Story
- ⭐ Game
- 🔄 Repeat
- ⏹ Stop

INTERNET CONNECTION REQUIRED FOR AUDIO DOWNLOAD.

To use this book with the Tag™ Reader you must download audio from the LeapFrog® Connect Application.
The LeapFrog Connect Application can be downloaded and installed at leapfrog.com/connect.

MR. PENCIL PRESENTS

DOODLEBURG
ROCKS!

written by Amy Keating Rogers
illustrated by Dave Walston

1

It was opening day of the Doodleburg
Fun Fair. Dot and Dash's band was going
to play.

"Wow, our band is really starting to heat up!" said Dot.

"Then let's cool off with some water balloons!" said Straight-Up Sue.

So they did.

Afterwards, Dot and Dash went looking for more musicians.

"We need a guitarist," said Dash.

"Let's ask Ziggy Zag," said Dot. "He's the best guitarist in Doodleburg!"

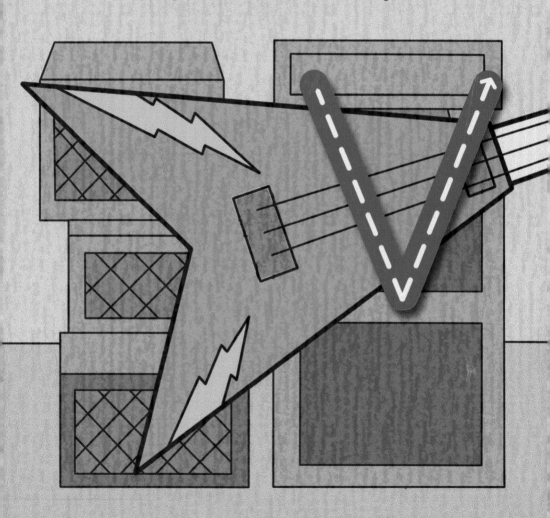

11

But Ziggy Zag had a problem. Pastel Paula the pirate had pilfered his treasure! Paula finally gave it back when they said she could join the band too.

14

"Piano, bass, guitar—our band is coming together!" said Dot.

But Dash thought something was missing.

"We need singers," he said.

"I can sing!" cried Pastel Paula.

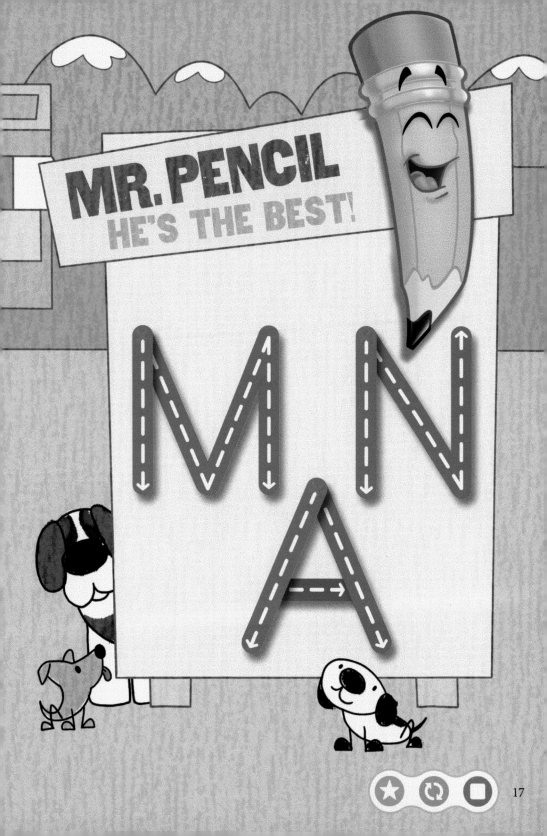

17

"Laaaaaa!" sang Paula.

"Wow, what power!" said Dot. "I think her voice shattered some records!"

"Some windows too," said Dash. "Let's call Curly Q. She has a flock of singing sheep."

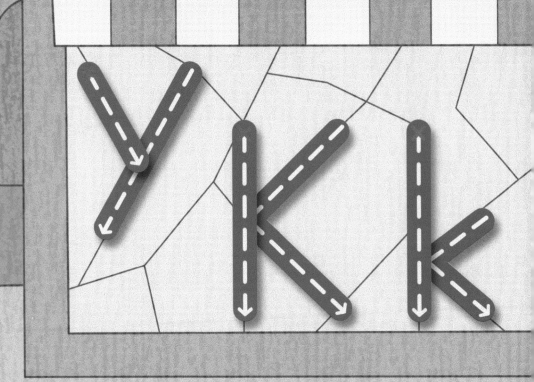

 "My sheep would love to sing," said Curly Q. "But it's two o'clock. Most of them are practicing."

"Practicing singing?" asked Dot.

"No! Practicing skateboarding!"

"Why would sheep be practicing skateboarding?" asked Dot.

"To get better at it!" said Curly Q. "They'll be done soon."

But after practice, the sheep skated away! The band chased after them.

"These sheep really rock and roll!" cried Ziggy Zag.

 "Piano, bass, guitar, singing sheep—now our band is really coming together!" said Dot.

But Dash thought something was still missing. "We need some dance moves," he said.

"Let's get Jimmy Jot," said Dot.
"He's the best dancer in Doodleburg."

So Jimmy Jot joined the band, and taught
them all to jitterbug.

"We still need a drummer," said Dash.

"Let's get Loopy Lou," said Dot. "He can drum circles around anyone in town."

They found Loopy Lou riding round and round at the Fun Fair.

31

"Piano, bass, guitar, singing sheep, dance moves, and a drummer—our band has come together!" said Dot.

They all warmed up for the big show.

"Our band will really be jumping tonight!" cried Dash.

Finally, it was time for the band to play. A huge crowd gathered in front of the Fun Fair stage.

The show began with Curly Q's sheep skateboarding spectacularly all over the stage.

Then, the band played. They were a smash hit! After that, they played at the Fun Fair every year. And their performances were always letter perfect!

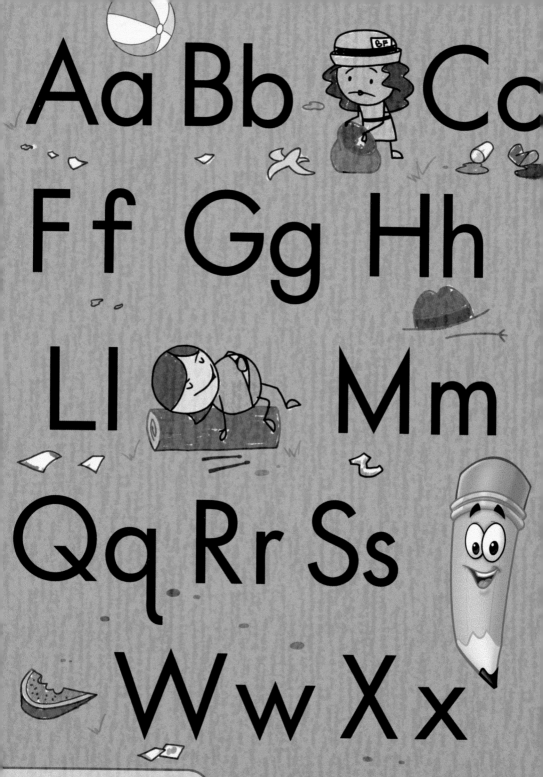

Aa Bb Cc
Ff Gg Hh
Ll Mm
Qq Rr Ss
Ww Xx